W9-BRJ-693

F
YOL   Yolen, Jane   c.1

        Shirlick Holmes and
         the case of the
         wandering wardrobe

DATE		
4.	3	
JAN 1 8 1983 3	FEB 1 4 1985 3	
FEB 1 1 1983	FEB 2 3 1988 3	
NOV 2 7 1984 3	NOV 2 1988 3	
DEC 2 0 1985	DEC 1 4 1988	
JAN 1 7 1986 3		

Department of Public Instruction

San Rafael School Library
BAHIA VISTA SCHOOL

No. ------------

Marin County, California

© THE BAKER & TAYLOR CO.

SHIRLICK HOLMES
AND THE CASE OF
THE WANDERING WARDROBE

BY **JANE YOLEN**
ILLUSTRATED BY **ANTHONY RAO**

Department of Public Instruction

San Rafael School Library
BAHIA VISTA SCHOOL

No.----------------

Marin County, California

COWARD, McCANN & GEOGHEGAN, INC. ✺ NEW YORK

For
F. N. Monjo
colleague, editor, friend
who breathed life into the past

Text copyright © 1981 by Jane Yolen
Illustrations copyright © 1981 by Anthony Rao
All rights reserved. This book, or parts thereof,
may not be reproduced in any form without permission
in writing from the publishers. Published simultaneously
in Canada by General Publishing Co. Limited, Toronto.
Library of Congress Cataloging in Publication Data

Yolen, Jane.
Shirlick Holmes and the case of the wandering
wardrobe.
SUMMARY: Shirli and her three friends determine
to solve the mystery of vanishing antiques that has
baffled the chief of police in their small town.
[1. Mystery and detective stories]
I. Rao, Anthony.   II.   Title.
PZ7.y78Sh   [Fic]   80-15406
ISBN 0-698-20498-0

Designed by Carolyn Craven
Second Impression
Printed in the United States of America

Contents

๛

1

Name Calling

You want to know a real twerpy name? Shirli. With an *i*.

Of course it's not my fault. No kid ever had a name that was her own fault. You're born and someone drops a name on you. You're much too small to argue. By the time you're grown, all you can hope for is a nickname.

So, what's a nickname for Shirli, with an *i*? Twirly Shirli. Pearly Shirli. Curli Shirli. (That's pretty funny in itself since my hair is long and dark and straight. *Very* straight.)

It was when my next-door neighbor and ex-best friend George Parker called me Girly Shirli that I decided to put my foot down. On his chest.

"Call me Shirlock," I said, sighting down my knee to his nose.

"Shir*lick*?"

Sometimes I think George is not too bright even though he gets A's in school, wins spelling bees, and can do crossword puzzles in ink.

"Listen, Georgie Pudgy," I said, because he's really skinny, "it's Shir*lock*. Like the famous detective. And that's what I'm going to be when I grow up."

George has already lived through my wanting to be a fighter pilot, a gymnast, and an astronaut. But that was all kid's stuff. This was for real.

George took my foot off his chest, and I must have slipped because suddenly I was sitting on the ground beside him. My ankle and bottom hurt, but I didn't cry. I never cry. I haven't cried, in fact, since I was seven and George kissed me. He'll never try *that* again.

"Listen yourself, Girly Shirli," he said. "You're never going to get a chance to grow up if you keep stepping on people's chests."

"Then I'll be a detective *before* I grow up."

George laughed and flicked the hair back out of his eyes. "You and who else?"

6

Thinking fast, I said, "Me and . . . and . . . and Gloria and Candy and Frances Bird." They were my best friends now. They all hated their names and boys as much as I did. That's how we became friends.

"Oh, terrific," said George, standing up and dusting off his back. He's kind of double-jointed. "Shirlick and the Sissies."

"And the Seekers!" I said, grabbing at his ankle and pulling him down again.

"*Oouf!*" he said. "Seekers! You girls couldn't find anything. Not even if it was in a paper bag with all your names on it in magic marker. Not even then."

"Could too."

"Could not."

"Could too." George was not great at arguing, so I always have to argue his way.

"Well, if you're so good, Shirlick . . ." he said and smiled.

"Shir*lock*!"

George smiled again. One of his slyest. "Then why don't you solve a *real* case. It's a case that even Chiefy is having problems with."

George's dad is chief of police in our town.

7

It's such a small town, we all call him Chiefy. Even George does—most of the time. Chiefy doesn't care. In fact, I think he likes it. And he likes all of us kids, too. When he's not solving cases, he's the school crossing guard. Actually, if you ask me, how he got Georgie Pudgy as a son is the biggest mystery around.

"Okay," I said. "We will. We *will* solve a real case."

"Who's we? The Glow Worm and Dandy Candy and Frances the Bird, I suppose."

Sometimes George is *real* dumb. I just nodded.

"Okay, then this is the case," said George. His voice suddenly got real quiet. He looked around for a moment, then down at his sneakers. I mean, *honestly*. There we were in the middle of his yard, under the tree-fort tree where George and I used to have tea parties when we were kids. Real *little* kids. Before the new development was built and other kids moved in on our block.

I looked around. There was no one for miles if you didn't count two women raking leaves far

down the street. But I moved over closer to George anyway. Just in case. You never really know in detecting.

"Okay," I said. "What is it?"

"Chiefy calls it *The Case of the Missing Furniture*," George whispered into my ear.

"Furniture!" I shouted. "Boy, is that ever twerpy. Who would want to take furniture? And who'd care if it's missing. Maybe a missing TV, but furniture?"

I stopped because George was making wild shushing motions with his hands and looking all around. But no one noticed us. And now there were three women and one older boy raking leaves. The boy was way across the street.

George whispered again. "It's a secret, Shirli. What kind of detective are you?"

I put my finger to my lips.

"This isn't ordinary furniture, Shirlick," he continued. He sounded so exasperated that this time I didn't even try and correct him. "It's antiques. Missing from the summer houses."

"Oh, summer houses!" I said, more loudly than I meant and quickly put my finger to my lips again. But after all, who cares about summer

10

houses and summer people anyway? They just come up on weekends in the spring and all of July and August and maybe one or two times in the Fall to watch the leaves turn. They don't do much for the town, and they complain a lot. At least that's what my grandmother, my dad's mom, says. And she should know. She's lived here all her life in the same house she was born in. We live there with her now.

But George continued. "Chiefy thought it was kids at first. That made him unhappy. You know, kids breaking in as a joke. He said we'd never had trouble with *his* kids before."

"But no one in Hansfield would . . ."

George nodded. "That's what made him so unhappy. There'd never been any real trouble before. Outsiders maybe. But not with our own kids."

I put my hands on my hips. "Who said it was Hansfield kids?"

George ran his fingers through his hair. "The summer people did. So Chiefy really started investigating then."

"And found . . ."

"And found out it wasn't just breaking into

11

houses. It was robbery." George rolled over onto his stomach. He plucked at some brownish grass. "And then they found Doc Kaiser's dog."

"Was he missing?"

"Who?"

"Doc Kaiser's dog, you twerp."

George sat up again and looked confused. "Missing? No he wasn't missing. But they found him."

Then I was confused. "Found him where?"

"Who?" asked George.

"Doc Kaiser's dog!" I said, real slowly, as if I were explaining things to a baby. Like I said, sometimes George can be real stupid.

George looked at me strangely. "I thought you knew. I mean, you always know most things that happen around town. But I guess maybe Chiefy has been keeping things real quiet. I heard him on the phone. By accident."

I moved closer. "Tell . . . Tell."

"Well Doc Kaiser's dog was found. In one of the robbed houses. He had been hit. Hard. On the head. And Maced, too. He still walks funny and chases parked cars. Doc is real upset. And

Chiefy is madder than I've ever seen him."

I nodded and scrunched my lips together. That made me mad, too. After all, Doc Kaiser's dog may be big and have an awful lot of teeth. But everyone knows he's a pushover for marshmallows and loves kids.

"Chiefy doesn't know what or who or how," George finished. "All those detective kind of questions. But when he's mad, well things aren't too terrific around our house."

If Chiefy was mad and I was mad, it was time to get other people mad about this, too. Not just keep it quiet. "Well, we'll find out what," I said, jumping up and towering over George. "And who. And how."

George stood up. Now we were eye to eye. "Bet you can't."

"Can."

"Can't."

"Can."

"Can't!"

"Can!" And that's how I got into the detective business.

2

The Seekers

We walked home together after school—Candy, Gloria, Frances Bird, and me.

That was nothing new. We always walked home together, ever since third grade. Except when it rained. Then we could always count on Candy's mother to come and get us.

Candy's mother always made little jokes about "My Candy might melt." If my Mom did that, I would die. But Candy would flutter her eyelashes and giggle. Then she and her mom would hug or wink at one another. Sometimes it almost made me sick.

But actually we were all kind of glad when Candy's mom came. None of us really likes to walk home in the rain. My Mom thinks cold rains makes you healthy or something. She's English. I don't think cold rain makes anyone healthy. Unless you're a plant, maybe.

This time when we walked home from school it was a nice warm Fall day. Some leaves coming down. Most of the lawns needed more raking, except Doc Kaiser's which was always clean as an operating room, my Mom says. And I told them all how we'd solve the mystery. "We'll call ourselves The Seekers!" I said.

"Like the singing group?" Candy added. That perked her up and she started humming. She loves things like rock groups and movie stars.

"I don't like it," said Frances Bird after a moment. Her mouth was set in that tight little way she had when something wasn't good enough for her.

But I know how to handle Frances Bird. "No," I said, "not a singing group. An English detective agency. Very upper *clahhss.*" Frances Bird likes my Mom. She comes over to listen to her stories about England all the time.

"Of course," said Frances Bird, smiling. "And we'll use our little grey cells."

Gloria stopped and put her hands on her hips. "Cells? Jail cells? I don't get it."

"Brain cells," said Frances Bird. "There's a famous detective in English mystery books who reasons everything out. He calls his brain his 'little grey cells.'"

Gloria nodded and seemed to be tucking that information away in her head along with everything else Frances Bird has ever told her. I swear, half of Gloria's education must come from Frances Bird. Maybe even three-quarters.

"Don't you think we sound like a singing group?" asked Candy, hopefully.

No one paid her any attention. She usually shuts up anyway after one question. But this time she was wound up as tight as her curls. (They're not natural, you know. Her mom makes her go for a permanent once a month.) "Do you think we should do this?" Her lower lip trembled. "Do you really and truly think we should? Don't you think it might be dangerous?"

"What's dangerous?" I asked. "What's danger?" I punched Frances Bird in the arm. "How can it be dangerous just to use our little grey cells?"

"Well, maybe a little dangerous?" asked Candy. "I mean, you said Doctor Kaiser's dog got hurt, didn't you? Didn't he?"

I was suddenly sorry I had mentioned that part. So I stopped and looked right at Candy, scrunching up my eyes a little. That usually makes her questions just fade away. "Just once," I said, "just once I wish you'd say something that wasn't a question."

"You do?"

Frances Bird twirled her right braid with her fingers. That meant she was thinking. There are never any arguments when Frances Bird does her thinking. She even wears a backpack for her books and pencils and papers and lunch so her hands are free for twirling her braids. "That dog," she began, and Gloria nodded along with her words. "That dog of Doc Kaiser's has *always* been strange. So he probably wasn't hit very hard. If he was hit at all. He might have walked into a tree. He's done that before. You can't make a dumb dog dumber by hitting it on the head."

"Right," said Gloria.

"Good thinking," I said. I didn't remind

Frances Bird that the dog had been found *in* the house. And I never mentioned the word Mace. You never do anything but agree when Frances Bird is thinking.

Frances Bird stopped twirling her braids and smiled and nodded her head.

So we all started walking again, and I told them the rest of the plan I had made.

"It seems to me that we ought to check the houses that were robbed," I said. "For clues."

"Okay," said Gloria. She was always ready for work. It was what she liked best. Not thinking—doing. She shifted her school books to one arm. "Let's go."

Frances Bird put her hand on Gloria's arm. She's so small and Gloria's so big, they make a funny pair. "We don't know which houses were robbed," she reminded Gloria.

"We don't, do we?" said Candy. She looked relieved.

"But we do!" I shouted. I felt like a magician. I pulled a list from my jeans pocket and held it in the air.

"Oh, dear," said Candy. It was her first statement of the day.

"Tee-rific," said Gloria, easily reaching over Frances Bird's head towards the list.

Candy made it into a little song. "Tee-he-rific, we'll find the crooks, just like they do in the comic books."

"*As,*" Frances Bird absent-mindedly corrected her. Then she stopped and began twirling her braid again. "Can we be sure that list is accurate?" she asked.

I smiled and nodded. "It's from George," I said.

"Oh, George," they all groaned together.

"He's not so bad," I said, remembering when he had been my best friend. "Besides, he *is* Chiefy's son."

"He's a pill," said Gloria.

"All boys are pills?" said Candy, not really looking for an answer.

"He copies off my paper," added Frances Bird.

"So does half the class," I said. "Excepting me. Besides he does not. He gets A's all by himself."

"They do? He does?" asked Candy.

"Don't be dumb," I said, dismissing Candy

and changing the subject. "There are eight houses on that list. The summer houses that got robbed. I notice none of the year-rounders' houses were touched. Guess we're not good enough for the thieves."

"We're not?" asked Candy.

"Don't be dumb," said Frances Bird. She took the list back from Gloria. "If there are eight places, we could each go to two this afternoon . . ."

Candy raised her hand. "Is *this* dumb? I think I have 4-H this afternoon?"

"Either you do or you don't," I mumbled.

"I do. I do." She sang it with a lot of trills.

Gloria snatched the list back from Frances Bird. She looked it over, squinching her eyes together and sounding out some of the harder names. "I can take Candy's houses, too," she said at last. "I don't mind. Really I don't."

"Yes," added Candy, patting her curls in place. "And if we let Gloria do them, maybe I can come after?"

Frances Bird twirled her braid faster than before. "It occurs to me that there might be real danger after all. Oh, not *real* danger, but at least some. And just in case, we'd better all go to-gether. It may be slower—but it *is* safer. Then if *anything* happens . . ." and she hesitated.

"I just remembered I have to practice my tap dancing after 4-H," said Candy. She was *very* positive and she wasn't singing.

"Nothing is going to happen," I said. I was even more positive. And I never sing. "This isn't TV, after all."

3

Checking the List

I was ready first. That's because I don't have to give my Mom a lot of explanations about where I'm going. She believes that kids my age should be *self-reliant*. She says that kids in England know all about that. It means doing things by yourself. Sometimes I wish she were more American. But mostly I like being self-reliant. I go a lot of places on my own.

So I wheeled my ten-speed to the corner where we all planned to meet. We meet a lot on that corner since we each live on one of the four streets that intersect there. My Mom used to call us the Corner Kids till I told her that was too *corny*.

Gloria was next, even though she had to come

the farthest. She lives way down at the end of the block in a real little house that doesn't even have a garage. But since there's just Gloria and her mom in the house and their car is so old it doesn't matter if snow and rain fall on it, I guess it doesn't bother them.

Frances Bird was last because, as usual, she took a lot of time to wave to her father and her brothers. Her father is a famous professor at the college, so he works at home most of the time. Her brothers are real pains. At least I think so. And their names are *worse* than Frances Bird's. One is called Bubba. And one is Willard A. But they're named after their mother's family. Their mother's dead, so they don't complain about their names. At least not very often.

Frances Bird waved and waved until Gloria sang out to her. That's when Frances Bird turned, saw us, and came fast. She's got a ten-speed, too, better than mine.

We decided to start at the top of the list because the first three houses were on the same road.

"Probably all hit the same day," said Frances Bird.

"Why would someone want to hit a house?" asked Gloria.

"That's detective talk," I explained. Gloria gets some of her education from me, too. "It means they were all robbed at the same time."

We got back on our bikes and pedaled off without talking. It's hard to go uphill and talk at the same time. And we didn't want to shout. After all, this was supposed to be a secret.

But the first house was empty. At least, it was almost empty.

"Nothing much here at all," I said, peering in the window from the porch. I did the looking because I was in charge. Besides, I think the other two were a little scared. "Just some old sofas and one table."

"Which means," said Frances Bird, twirling her braid, "that they took everything."

"Maybe there wasn't much to begin with," said Gloria.

"Don't be *dumb*," I said. "These are summer people. That means they're rich. Think of it, they each have at least two houses. This house for the summer and somewhere else for the rest

24

of the year."

Gloria nodded. "I guess you're right. I was just trying to use my little green cells."

"Grey," said Frances Bird. "*Grey.*"

The next two houses were about a hundred yards apart down the road. They were pretty empty, too, though each looked freshly painted. I guess our house hasn't been painted for years. Each time I looked in the windows, and Gloria and Frances Bird stayed on the lawn. But they kept a good watch on the road, ready to let me know if they saw any cars coming.

After the third house, we sat down. The lawn was prickly because of the dried grass and partially covered with leaves. I took out the list. "What next?" I said. I knew where I wanted to go, but Frances Bird likes to make decisions.

"There's one more house on this road," pointed out Frances Bird, twirling her braid.

"It's not on the list," I said. "So it hasn't been robbed."

"Not yet," said Frances Bird.

We looked at each other. Frances Bird and I looked sly. Gloria looked puzzled.

"Think like a thief," I said to Gloria.

"If three why not four," prompted Frances Bird.

"I get it!" shouted Gloria. "Let's go." She got up and on to her bike so fast, she beat Frances Bird and me to the fourth house by a full minute.

By now it was starting to get dark. Oh, not nighttime-dark, but fall-afternoon-dark. With clouds. My stomach growled. That was hunger, of course, not fear. We left the bikes on the lawn, and all three of us ran up onto the porch. It was hard seeing into the house.

"I can't tell if anything is there," I said.

"The light's wrong," complained Frances Bird.

Gloria didn't say anything, but she leaped off the porch and fell onto her knees. She was up again in an instant, running around the back of the house.

"Come on," we heard her call.

By the time we got around back, Gloria was standing by a basement bulkhead door. It was yawning wide open. "There!" said Gloria. "That sure is heavy. I babysat here once. The people had me close the bulkhead door so their kids

26

wouldn't fall in. I remembered it was here."

"Tee-rific," I said. "Let's go."

"No!" said Frances Bird. "We are positively *not* going in there. It's too dark and there won't be lights because summer people always turn off their electricity in the winter."

Gloria looked disappointed.

I felt disgusted. "We *have* to go in. And if you two won't, I'll go in myself. That's what a real detective would do."

They followed me in. We held hands and crept about in the dark. It was like being blind and in a new country. Nothing seemed in the right place.

"Ow," Gloria whispered. The dark always makes people whisper. "I've stumbled into something."

"Me!" I said. It hurt, but I refused to cry. Even if no one could have seen me in the dark.

We could almost hear Frances Bird twirling her braid. "Shh," she said.

"Why shh?" I said. "There's no one here. In fact, I don't think there's *anything* here. It's the cleanest basement I've ever stumbled about in."

"Shhhh," said Frances Bird again. "There *is* someone here. Upstairs. I can hear him."

Just then the door at the top of the cellar stairs creaked open. A light shone down. It was a shaky little light.

Thinking quickly, I shouted in my deepest voice: "It's the thieves. Quick. Someone catch them before they get away." I hoped to scare them.

But Gloria took me at my word. Before anyone else could move, she dashed up the stairs yelling. She grabbed the flashlight and flashed it up and down. I thought she was shaking so bad she couldn't hold the light still. Turns out she was just trying to find the thief's face. It took her a while. It was the longest while I have ever lived through.

4

An Arresting Situation

The flashlight found a face at last.

It was Candy.

"You twerp!" I shouted, relieved. I ran up the stairs.

"I am?"

I shouted all the way up. "What are you doing here? You scared us half to death. Why didn't you say something?" And all the while my heart was thumping from all that running and all that shouting.

Frances Bird came up after me. Then hand in hand we all went through the first floor rooms. It was amazing how much brighter it seemed, even though it was getting dark outside. I guess that is because there is *nothing* darker than a strange basement with three new detectives in it. Was I glad to be able to see again. And what I saw was . . .

"Nothing!" said Gloria. "There's nothing here at all. No sofas. No chairs. No drapes. No rugs."

Frances Bird twirled her braid. "If there's nothing here, the thieves must have really stripped this place bare."

"They left the door open, too, I think?" added Candy.

"So that's how you got in," I said.

"I did?"

We ignored her and sat on the floor. There was nowhere else to sit. "This calls for a *lot* of grey cells," I said.

Candy sat, too, crossing her legs in front of her and smoothing her skirt over her knees.

Gloria took a strand of her hair and tried to twirl it like a braid. Maybe her hair was too short. Or maybe her thinking was too short. But after a while, she shook her head. "My little grey cells can't figure *anything* out," she said.

"What can't you figure out?" asked Frances Bird.

"Why they took some things from the other

houses but *everything* from this house," Gloria said.

I was glad she asked that because that was the question that was bothering me. But I wasn't about to let anyone know I couldn't figure it out.

"I mean," Gloria continued, "the furniture in this house wasn't all that great. The TV was only a black and white."

"Well they must have been in a hurry," said Frances Bird, her hand on her braid. "Because they left so fast, they forgot to lock the door."

And I added, "Only who'd have been dumb enough to figure they might do something like that?"

We all looked at Candy.

"I would?" she asked.

Just then I heard something and put my finger to my mouth. "Shh," I said. "We have company. There's a car outside."

"The thieves," whispered Candy. "Are they back to finish off this place?"

"They *have* finished off this place," I said.

"Maybe they came back to lock the door?" asked Candy.

It was the only reasonable thing she had said so far. And then she added, "They'll know we're here. Your bikes are all over the front lawn."

Now why did she have to sound so positive?

We crawled behind the door, all huddled together. It kept us warm, but none of us thought it would keep us safe. Not really.

A car door slammed. I heard a gruffish voice saying, "Come on, Boy."

Footsteps came up the stairs, across the porch, up to the door. Keys clanked together. The door opened with a creak.

"There they are, Dad," said George. "I see Candy's shoe. She's the only one I know who wears Mary Janes."

"Okay, girls," said Chiefy. "Time to get up."

We stood up, feeling a little silly and a lot safer.

"Aw, Chief Parker," I said in my sweetest voice. He's my neighbor, after all. We're old friends. "We were just trying to help."

"Help, schmelp," he said. "According to the law, you girls have done what is known as Breaking and Entering. Not to mention Trespassing.

So I am going to have to arrest you and take you to jail."

Candy gasped.

Gloria and Frances Bird were silent.

But I knew it was time for straight talk. "Oh, come on, Chiefy. I know this town doesn't have a jail. Just your house. And we didn't break into anything. Both the cellar door and the front door were already open. And we didn't break anything here because, as you can see, there's nothing here to break."

The others breathed loudly. I guess it was agreement. I watched Chiefy's face. He was having trouble keeping from laughing. That was a good sign. I can always make him laugh. "You see, *I* figure this house has been hit, too, Chiefy. The thieves really picked it over. There's nothing left here at all. But you missed it. It's not on your list. And *I* found it."

The girls mumbled something. Frances Bird kicked my shin.

"*We*," hissed Frances Bird.

"*We* found it," I added quickly. "We. The Seekers. Shirlick Holmes and the Seekers." I meant Shir*lock*. George smiled.

Chiefy laughed out loud then. And I began to relax.

"Picked it over," he said. "You think thieves picked this one over? Well, little girls, I'll show you picked-it-over." He shoved us all out of the door and locked it behind him. Then he pointed.

There, in front of the house, right close to where we had left our bikes, was a big FOR SALE sign.

"There is nothing here because the people have moved, not because the place has been robbed," said Chiefy. "The one thing detectives should never do is jump to conclusions," he added. "And you, Miss Shirli, have a long way to go to become a bona fide detective."

George let out a whoop, and I shook my fist at him.

"Enough," said Chiefy to George. Then he put his hand on my head and said to all of us, "Get on your bikes and meet me at headquarters. We have some serious talking to do about your entering—if not breaking—into this house. And I'll want your parents in on it, too."

With that, he and George went down the porch steps and got into the car. Chiefy gunned it onto the road. George waved once from the front seat.

Glumly we all hopped onto our bicycles. We were too upset even to argue. We just rode back in silence, all the way home.

5

A Warning from Chiefy

We were—and we weren't—under arrest. I was right when I reminded Chiefy that our town has no jail. But being in his living room with our parents staring at us made us *feel* in jail.

Chiefy did most of the talking. "The girls wanted to help out, and that makes me proud," he began. "Proud that these are our kids. Proud that they care about the town."

I started to smile and shifted from one foot to the other. Candy, sitting on the sofa next to her mother, her legs crossed like a lady, folded and unfolded her hands. Gloria, standing behind her mother who was also on the sofa, slumped and tried to make herself small. Frances Bird, perched on the arm of the easy chair in which her father sat, kept her hand on his arm. Her braids hung down her back.

"Yes," Chiefy continued, "proud that they care about the law. *But . . .*" And then he slammed one big fist on his knee. "They broke the law while trying to help the law. *And I don't like that!*"

"Now, Chief," said my Mom, who was standing next to me, leaning against the wall. "They didn't *really* break the law. Besides, they probably didn't know such a law existed."

"Ignorance . . ." began Chiefy.

". . . of the law is no excuse," finished Frances Bird's father quietly. "Of course. Of course."

Chief looked over at him to see if Professor Baylor was mocking him, but he wasn't, so Chiefy began again. "More important, it was *just plain dangerous.*"

"Dangerous. Oh, my," said Candy's mother. "Candy, thank your stars your father is at work right now. If he were here, I don't know what he'd say." Her hand fluttered to her neck and she began toying with her pearls. Her other hand had a dragon-hold on Candy.

My Mom just shook her head and winked at Gloria's mom.

But Professor Baylor cocked his head. "Dangerous? If it was dangerous, then to get involved was plain stupidity. And *that* I won't countenance."

"Of course it was dangerous," said Chiefy. "Whoever these furniture thieves are, they mean business. Big business."

"You mean . . . the Mafia?" asked Candy's mother.

"Well, not quite as big as all that," admitted Chiefy.

Gloria's mom turned and winked back at my Mom.

"But they already Maced Doc Kaiser's dog," put in George.

"Wow, *Maced!*" said Gloria, turning to look at me. Her mouth made the words "You didn't tell us that!" but she didn't speak them out loud.

I shrugged.

Chiefy continued, "And what if our little girls got Maced? How would you girls feel then?"

Everyone started to talk at once then. Except me. I felt as if everyone blamed me for things.

40

But what things? After all, nothing had happened. Why was everyone so upset?

"As of now," said Chiefy, "You girls are officially *off this case!*" He spoke loud enough to shut everyone up. Except for George, who laughed.

At George's laugh, the Chief put his hand on George's head which stopped the laugh between one ha and the next. "But in case you girls are still interested in some cops-and-robbers action . . ."

"We *are*," I said. "We *are*."

No one else said anything. My voice echoed in Chiefy's living room.

"Then I have a plan, though I am not waiting for volunteers," said Chiefy. He stood up and looked meaningfully at all of us and nodded at his wife, who stood in the doorway with a tray of lemonade and cookies. "Instead of jail—which would make this house pretty crowded—I'm going to have you girls police the areas around the summer houses for one school week. Five days."

"Police work. Tee-rific," said Gloria. "Clues and grey cells. Let's do it."

41

"Should I?" asked Candy, looking at her mother.

"You're *all* going to do it," said Chiefy. "That's an order."

The parents nodded.

Frances Bird cleared her throat and her mouth got real small. "You did say *police* the area, didn't you, Chief Parker?"

He smiled. "I did, Frances Bird."

"You mean police as in pick-up-the-area?" said Frances Bird.

"She's a smart one all right, Professor," said the Chief to Frances Bird's father. "That's right, little lady."

If there's one thing Frances Bird can't stand, it's being called a little lady. She pulled her shoulders back and stood up. "Which means we won't be detectives or deputies or anything else except garbage persons."

"And I'm sending George along to keep an eye on you. Keep you *all* out of trouble. Especially you, Shirli Holmes."

"Me?" I squeaked. But the meeting was over, and Mrs. Parker's cookies are always the greatest. I ate four.

6

Police Work

Don't let anyone ever tell you that police work is fun. It's not. It's bor-ing. At least this kind of police work sure was.

This kind means bending over a lot. And picking up a lot. Stuff most kids hate. Especially me. On a nice Fall day I'd rather be out riding my bike. Or climbing rocks. Or playing touch football. But this kind of police work was real work. Finding trash and throwing it in garbage bags.

We hated it.

We started at the first house that had been robbed. On the lawn, half buried in leaves, were two old beer cans, lollipop sticks, a soda can, and Juicy Fruit gum wrappers.

"Why so many Juicy Fruit gum wrappers?"

I asked. "It loses its taste fastest."

"But it tastes best," said Frances Bird. "I know because I did a special taste poll for extra credit in math. My graph clearly showed that more kids liked the taste."

Candy, who was not allowed to chew gum because of her braces, said nothing. And Gloria, who was hard at work, didn't hear us.

"Ugh," called out Gloria, standing up and holding something dark and brown and disgusting between her thumb and forefinger. She made a face.

"Is it dead?" I asked.

"Very," she said.

"Gross," cried out Candy.

Frances Bird took one look and shook her head. "It's just a cigar," she said.

"Keep working!" shouted George who was taking his job very seriously. Too seriously.

The next day was the same, only the house was different. And *some* of the trash. No beer cans this time and a different soda can. One soda bottle. Lots of lollipop sticks. And another well-chewed, very dead cigar.

"And Juicy Fruit wrappers!" called out Gloria as she pounced on each one.

"*Wonderful*," I said sarcastically. Then I thought about becoming a firewoman instead.

Frances Bird twirled her braid and looked like she was thinking, but she said nothing.

Candy missed this session. She had a piano recital.

"Keep working!" shouted George.

Days three and four were the same. Lots of beer bottles and an empty cigarette carton were the only variations. And six broken matchbox cars with no front wheels or back. And . . .

"A cigar!" shouted Gloria, pointing. This time none of us even bothered to pick it up, though we kicked it around a bit with our shoes. Even Candy.

"Keep working!" shouted George.

We ignored him, got on our bikes, and rode home. George was left to tote the plastic bag full of junk to the dump. I hope he hated every minute of it.

The last day, the fifth school day, of our police work we had to go to a new part of town. We had cleaned up the houses we had "broken and entered," but Chiefy still wouldn't let us off. Five days he had said, and five days it remained. He found us a summer home that had what looked like a mile of lawn—front and back. This time, though, George was supposed to help. He had done something bad at home—he wouldn't tell us what—and as a punishment his dad said he had to work alongside of us.

We all started in the back. Every time George slowed down, one or another of us would shout, "Keep working!" After a while, he got the picture and went to police the front lawn by himself.

"Now we can relax," I said, sitting down on the back steps and running my fingers through my hair.

"We can?" asked Candy. She stood there looking silly with a lollipop stick in each hand.

Frances Bird stopped, too, a cigar, all chewed and gooey, between her fingers. She flipped it at Gloria who caught it and threw it back. Frances Bird popped the cigar into our plastic trash bag and came over to sit next to me.

Candy sat down on my other side and brushed

her hands together briskly, trying to wipe off the dirt.

But Gloria kept on working. She called out as she put things into the bag, like a chant or a song: "Juicy Fruit wrapper, lollipop stick, Juicy Fruit wrapper, lollipop stick . . ."

We all started saying it with her. "Juicy Fruit wrapper, lollipop stick, Juicy Fruit wrapper . . ."

And Frances Bird's braid started twirling. Faster and faster and faster it went.

"*Stop!*" I shouted suddenly, grabbing the braid and yanking it like a bellrope.

"Ow!" screamed Frances Bird. "what are you doing? I haven't finished thinking."

"Well, I have," I said. "Those are all clues. They've been in front of us all the time: the Juicy Fruit wrappers and the lollipop sticks and the cigar."

"The cigar?" asked Gloria and Frances Bird. I swear they sounded just like Candy.

I nodded at them. "This police work has paid off."

"It has?" asked Candy.

"*It sure has*," I said. "Boy, we really are Seekers."

7

New Girl in Town

"We did it!" shouted Gloria. Then she suddenly looked confused. After all, she didn't know what we had done. Only I knew. But that didn't stop her from shouting and jumping up and down. "Did it, did it, did it."

We all joined her.

Our shouting brought George around in a run. He saw us jumping up and down, even Candy, who was applauding politely.

"Did what?" asked George. And then he added, angrily, "You're not working."

We all shut up, stopped jumping, and winked at each other and giggled. We knew it would drive George crazy.

"Girls! Giggling! Secrets!" George said. He threw a handful of lollipop sticks at the bag and missed. "See if I care," he said and walked back slowly towards the front of the house.

"Oh, I get it, I think?" said Candy in a loud, breathless voice. "*Clues!*"

"Shhhhhhhh," Frances Bird and Gloria and I said together.

But George had heard. He turned back. "What clues? Which? Who found 'em? Where? What are they?" He sounded like a bad imitation of Candy.

"Don't say anything," I hissed at the others.

"We don't *know* anything," whispered Frances Bird back to me.

I ignored her and smiled at George. "Won't tell," I said. "After all, you thought we were the Sissies."

"Seekers," said George.

"And you've been bullying us for days," I added.

"Just following orders," said George.

"And you told your father where we were and got us into trouble in the first place," I said.

"That's not fair," said George. "I was worried about you."

"Well . . ." I began.

"I bet you don't know *anything*," said George.

"Do."

"Don't."

"Do."

"Don't."

"Only *girls* can know," I said. "Only members of the Seekers."

George looked over his shoulder as if to be sure none of his friends could hear him. That was a real twerpy thing to do. After all, he was alone. No boys for miles. "Then let me be a member of the club," he said at last.

"It's not a club," said Frances Bird.

"It's just for girls," said Gloria.

"And you don't think you're a girl, do you?" asked Candy.

I laughed out loud and clapped Candy on the back. "That's it. Oh, Candy, you're a genius."

"I am?"

I pulled the girls around into a tight huddle and told them why Candy was a genius. They all agreed. Then we faced George, but *I* got to tell him because it was *my* idea.

"Sure we'll let you into the Seekers—and into the secret—but on one condition."

George folded his arms and tried to look cool. He looked eager and hungry instead. "Okay," he said, but his mouth moved in a funny way, and he unfolded his arms and smoothed down his hair with both hands. Then he put his hands into his pockets and licked the corner of his mouth. "Okay," he repeated.

"The one condition is—you have to become an honorary girl," I said.

"Oh, brother!" said George. He took his hands out of his pockets and walked off.

"Or no secret!" Frances Bird called after him in her sternest voice. "And no clues." Candy giggled.

George turned halfway back. He said, "Well, what does an honorary girl have to do? Wear a skirt?"

"Don't be a twerp," I said. "Look around. How many girls do you see wearing skirts here?"

We all looked. Gloria and I were wearing blue jeans. Frances Bird was wearing overalls. Only Candy wore a skirt. Ever.

"Then I guess I'll have to wear long hair," said George.

"You'd have to *cut* your hair to get it as short as mine," said Gloria.

51

Frances Bird twirled her braid. "All you really have to do is recite a pledge," she said.

I tried to look daggers at her. This was supposed to be *my* idea.

"What kind?" asked George.

Frances Bird looked desperately at me.

"A pledge," I said, stalling and thinking hard. "That . . . that you swear to try harder to be as good as a girl in all things."

Frances Bird added, "And to think things through with your heart as well as your mind."

"And not to always tease other people," said Candy. "Especially other girls."

Gloria looked down at her hands, then up at George. "And to be accepting of other people when they are different from you."

Putting his hand over his heart, George gulped and said, "I so pledge." Then he looked at me. "So what's the secret?" he asked.

"Yeah," said the other girls to me. "We want to know, too."

8

Clues Worthy

"We have all the clues," I said. "And it's all so simple, really. Look at all the junk we've found. There are a lot of different things. But three keep coming up over and over again."

Frances Bird jumped right in. "Juicy Fruit wrappers," she said.

I nodded.

Gloria followed. "And lollipop sticks."

I nodded again.

"And a sticky, smelly, really gross cigar. Well chewed." Two positive statements in a row from Candy.

But George wasn't convinced. "So . . ." he said.

"Think," I said. "Use those little grey cells." I lowered my voice and everyone moved in closer to me. "The summer houses are left in the fall and winter. No one much cleans the lawns until late spring. But they are really well kept up when the summer people are home. So, anything on the lawn had to have gotten there *after* the summer people went away. If someone came to the house and stood around a while, looking the place over, planning to rob it, they might drop their trash. And it wouldn't be picked up until next spring. All these things are clues to the people who want to rob this house—next!"

"You mean," George added, "there were three robbers. Mr. Juicy Fruit . . ."

I nodded. "Call him JF."

"Mr. Lolly and Mr. Cigar," George concluded.

I smiled. "I told you he wasn't so bad."

George smiled back and punched me on the arm. "For a girl," he added.

We all jumped on him then and tickled and pounded him until he gave up. Then we all untangled and sat on the ground with red and gold leaves in our hair and on our shirts. Candy picked dirt from her knee.

Frances Bird held both her braids in her hands

and looked like she was considering. Finally she said. "They *might* be clues and they *might not*. But either way, I don't think they will be enough to convince Chiefy."

"I agree," said George, which was the first time on record he and Frances Bird ever agreed on anything. But since George knows his dad better than any of us, we agreed, too. Besides, we all secretly liked the idea that the Seekers might solve the case without the help of the police.

"Why don't we have a stake-out?" asked George.

Of course I was about to suggest that and punched George in the arm because he beat me to it. But then *I* got to explain what it meant. We would take turns keeping an eye on this house as late at night as we dared. That way, when the robbers came and stole something, we could ride on our bikes to Chiefy's while the robbers were inside.

Gloria, George, and I volunteered for the first night. I wouldn't have missed it for the world. George felt he had to prove himself worthy of being a girl. And Gloria, of course, likes to *do* something.

So we met at the corner after dinner and rode quietly to the summer house. I had told my Mom I was going to Gloria's. So had George. And Gloria had said she was going to be with me. White lies don't really count, you know. And it was for a good cause.

We remembered how Candy and Chiefy had seen our bikes, so this time we hid them behind a stand of birch trees. Then we hid with them.

It got colder. It got darker. And it got quieter. Two cars went by, but no one stopped.

My teeth began to chatter. "I vote we make this a stake-*in*," I said.

"A stake-in?" asked George. "Never heard of it."

But Gloria nodded at me. Her teeth were chattering, too.

"A stake-in," I said, "means we do our stake-out from *in*side the house."

"Isn't that dangerous?" asked George.

"If you're a girl, you don't worry about danger," I said.

"You only worry about cold," mumbled George, but he followed.

The front door was locked. We knew because we tried it. There was no basement door. But we did find a basement window open. George went in first because he had been smart enough to remember a flashlight. Gloria was next because she was colder than I was. I came last and put the window back up so no one could tell we were there.

We were in a nice playroom. There was a TV and a stereo, but without electricity neither one could work. We knew because we tried them. So we made our way upstairs with the help of the flashlight.

We were just settling down on the sofa when a funny noise quieted us.

It was a car.

I went over to the window and peered out. The car came into the driveway, but something was funny. It was pretty dark out now, and the car had no lights on.

"Oh-oh," I said, "it's the robbers."

"I thought that was what we wanted," said Gloria.

I was glad she couldn't see my face in the dark. It felt all hot and flushed. "That *was* what we wanted—when we were on the outside," I said. "Only we're on the inside now. So we don't want them anymore."

"Then we'd better *do* something," Gloria said frantically.

"What?" I answered sensibly.

"Hide," said George and turned. Then he added, "And no flashlight." That was easy for him to say since he had the only flashlight.

George and Gloria both headed out of the room towards the hall closet we had seen on our way into the living room. I heard them arguing in loud whispers over who had gotten to it first. But then I realized I'd better stop listening to them and start finding somewhere to hide myself. Hand over hand, I went along the wall and found a door. I went through it and smacked into a bed. Then a little way farther I found a standing wardrobe. We have one like it at home—a big, moveable wooden closet. I opened the door and climbed in.

Before I closed the door, I listened carefully. I heard two things: the hall closet door shut and

footsteps stumbling down the basement stairs. Probably Gloria, I thought, since she's so much clumsier than George. I hoped she could find the basement window, get out, find her bike, and get away without being seen. I hoped that hope harder than anything because the next sound I heard was the front door. *Someone* had managed to unlock it. And this time I *knew* it wasn't Chiefy.

With a silent prayer, I closed the wardrobe closet. I hoped no one else heard its super-loud click.

9

In the Wardrobe

It was real dark in that wardrobe. Stuffy, too. I don't like dark stuffy places. People who are scared of being in small, closed-in places have something called *claustrophobia*. I know because my Mom has it.

Well I don't have that, but I think I now have closet-phobia from being in that wardrobe.

I kept my nose right up to the crack of the door to get as much air as possible.

But I also kept my ear there, too. If you think that's impossible, try it.

Of course I was so busy trying to breathe and trying to hear what was going on, I didn't have time to get scared. Well, not *real* scared. Not at first. That came later.

I heard muffled footsteps. I heard whispers

and one deep laugh. I heard stompings and mutterings and sounds of scrapings. And then I heard nothing. Nothing at all.

I don't know why, but the silence was worse than the noise. That's when I started to get scared.

I didn't dare cough or sniff or rub my nose. I didn't dare wipe my eyes or call for help. And I sure didn't dare cry. Not that I would, of course. I never cry. I didn't dare whimper or whistle up courage. I just didn't dare.

My stomach felt as if there were something hard inside it. I could hardly breathe. And just as I was about to do something, anything, to break the silence, I heard voices again. Loud and clear.

"Keep that flashlight down, dummy," came a voice that was low and gravelly, as if its owner smoked too much. I decided that was Mr. Cigar.

"It's down, Boss, down," was the answer in a flat voice that sounded like it came from a nose and not a mouth. That had to be Lolly because it's hard to talk and suck on a lollipop at the same time.

"Down," came a third voice with a high,

crackling echo. That had to be JF, chewing his gum and cracking it. Obviously he couldn't do that and walk and talk at the same time. Too dumb.

They were so close, I could have touched them if I wanted to. Or they could have touched me—if they had known I was there. And I got so scared then, I think I would have opened the wardrobe door and given myself up to them just to stop my heart from pounding so hard. I even had my hand on the door to push it open when I heard them move away.

"You check all the closets," said Mr. Cigar. "And Dummy here will move the furniture I pick out."

"Yea, Boss, yea," said Lolly.

The closets! But George was hiding in a closet. What if they saw him? What if they found him? Would they Mace him like they Maced Doc Kaiser's dog? Would they hit him on the head? Would they kill . . . but before I could think of any more horrors, the voices came close to me again.

"I like the looks of this wardrobe," said Mr. Cigar. "Good wood. Oak. Sturdy, but with fine decoration. Like to check the inside. Dummy, open it."

Open it! They meant me. I held onto the door, my fingers clamped around a little piece of wood that locked the door into place.

"It's stuck, Boss," Dummy called out, yanking again.

"Don't fiddle with it then," came Mr. Cigar's voice. "If you break it, the value will just go down."

Mine, too, I thought miserably.

Mr. Cigar continued. "I'll deal with that later. In good light. *And* with the proper tools. Just move it. It'll take two of you. Hey," he called out. "Come here and help the dummy move this wardrobe."

The wardrobe was suddenly picked up and tipped on to its side. I had to hold the clothes rod to keep from falling out into their laps.

"Boss, this is kinda heavy," said Lolly.

"Yea," added JF.

The answer was muffled as if Mr. Cigar was away in a different room. "That's oak for you. Heaviest wood around."

I was angry for just a minute. After all, I only

weigh 83 pounds soaking wet. But my fear overcame my anger just as fast. We bumped along for a few moments with Lolly and JF grunting and groaning and complaining. Down stairs and over a lawn was my guess. Then I was upright again and an awful screech filled my ears as the wardrobe was pushed along something metal. A truck? Then the wardrobe was still and everything was silent again.

Minutes went by without a sound. Then I heard some faint gruntings and groanings and another awful screech. Something else big was sliding along the floor of the truck.

Silence again.

That second silence was shorter. The noise and grunts and slides led immediately into a third silence. It was obvious that the wardrobe (and me in it) was on a truck and other furniture was being added. If I wanted to get away, find my bike, and ride home I had to get out at a silent time.

It was now or never.

I pushed the door gently.

Nothing happened.

I pushed again harder.

The door moved a bit and struck a wall.

I pushed with all my might, but the door was stuck. And then I knew. The wardrobe was pushed up against the side of the truck. I would never be able to open the door. I was truly and awfully caught. It was not a game any more. There was no way out.

I wondered what Mr. Cigar would do to me when he found me. Because he was going to find me. Of that I had no doubt at all.

10

A Long Dark Night

My closet-phobia got worse. There are only two things you can do if you are shut up in a wardrobe in the back of a truck being carted off to somewhere unknown by a gang of robbers. One is to go to sleep. The other is to think.

There wasn't enough room to lie down. There was just enough room to sit or kneel.

And I had to go to the bathroom. And to be honest, I was too scared to go to sleep.

So I thought.

They weren't good thoughts. They weren't happy thoughts. I guess they weren't even very original thoughts. But this is what they were.

First I thought about George. I wondered if he had been found. I sure hoped not. He really *is* my good friend. Maybe even my best friend.

Even if he is a boy. And it was my fault he was in that closet.

Then I thought about Gloria. I wondered if she had gotten out the window. I wondered if she had found her bike in the dark and made it back home. I wondered if she had told her mother. Or my mother. Or Chiefy. I knew Gloria can always be counted on to do the right thing. But she has to be told what that right thing is. So maybe she just went home to bed. She sure had every right to do that and not tell anyone anything. She was probably tired after the bike ride. And scared. She had told her mom a lie. She had done breaking-and-entering on another house. So if she was tired and scared and unhappy and went right to bed, it was my fault.

I thought about Frances Bird and Candy. They were lucky not to be here tonight. Not that they really wanted to be. But if I had decided they were to be first at the stake-out, they would have been. Then they would have been caught, too. In a closet or in a wardrobe or Maced or hit. And it would have been my fault.

I thought about Chiefy, who cared about us kids. He had warned us about the danger. But

I had ignored his warning. And now his son, his only son, was about to be caught and hit and Maced by robbers. And another house would be broken into. And his reputation and his son would be gone. And it was all my fault.

I thought about Mom and Dad and Gram. They would all be wondering why I wasn't home. They would call Gloria's and find out I had never gone there. They would call all my friends and find me missing. They would call Chiefy and find out George was missing, too. So they'd know I lied to them, and they would be unhappy. And mad. And they'd know I was in danger. And they'd be scared. And they'd never find me again. And it was all my fault that they'd be sad and mad and unhappy and miserable and lonely all the rest of their lives.

And then I started thinking about me. And just as I got to that subject, a door slammed close by. The truck started up. And the rattling and the bumping and jouncing and banging kept me from thinking.

But it didn't keep me from falling asleep.

11

Auctioned Off

I woke up hours later. At least I guessed it was hours later because my stomach was growling. It was hunger—not fear. My only fear was that my stomach growling would reach the ears of Mr. Cigar, Lolly, or JF.

The truck had stopped. There was no more bouncing. In fact, I wondered if I was still on the truck at all. I could hear a lot of mumbling voices and then, suddenly, one real loud one. It was so loud, I realized it was over a microphone.

The voice was saying, "And a sudden late shipment has brought in some really fine pieces that were not available for your earlier inspection, ladies and gentlemen. Like this nice wardrobe. Good wood. Oak. Sturdy, but not without fine decoration."

I was still half asleep, but I had heard those same words somewhere before. Then I remembered. That was exactly what Mr. Cigar had said about the wardrobe back at the house.

"A fine wardrobe," continued the microphone voice. "A classic. Look at its lines. Why, in New York City such a piece would go for several hundreds of dollars. So what am I bid?"

Suddenly I was awake—and mad. He was auctioning my wardrobe off. And me! Of course he didn't know I was in it. But he did know he had stolen it.

I thought about popping right out then and there. But I had another thought. Actually, I was getting pretty good at thinking. All that time in the dark by myself. And what I thought was this: if I popped out now, I might find myself in the middle of a robbers' auction. *All* the people at this sale might be robbers. Hadn't there been a kind of chuckling when he said "a sudden late shipment"? So just in case, I scrunched myself together a little more and held onto my knees. Both my feet were sound asleep, but my mind was wide awake. My body wanted to get out of the wardrobe, but my brain warned me that I just didn't dare.

The bidding began. I heard a low voice call out, "Fifty dollars."

"Fifty dollars for this beautiful wardrobe, this excellent piece? Why that's a steal."

That's when I was sure I was right. The whole audience was a bunch of crooks. Because they laughed out loud then.

"Sixty," came a familiar voice. I tried to place it.

"Seventy-five," boomed the low answer.

"Eighty," returned the familiar voice. I tried and tried to remember who it was.

"One hundred," came a high woman's voice.

The auctioneer took over again with the microphone. "The bid is one hundred from the lovely lady in the red hat," he said. "Do I hear more?"

"One hundred and five," came that voice again. I had to see who it was. It seemed familiar yet, muffled by the door, it was disguised just enough so I could not place it. I pushed the wardrobe open just a crack. The click of the door opening was smothered by the auctioneer shouting over the microphone.

"Come on, my friends. This is too much of a bargain to be let go."

"One hundred and twenty-five," said the original boomer.

"A steal," reminded the auctioneer.

"One hundred and thirty," came the familiar voice.

And then I knew. "*Chiefy!*" I yelled and tried to stand up in the wardrobe and push the door open. But my feet were asleep and my knees were cramped. I spilled out of the wardrobe and tumbled to the floor.

Everyone in the place stood up and started talking at once. I looked up at the stage where the auctioneer stood. He was a short, pudgy man chewing on a cigar. His mouth dropped open and the cigar fell on the floor.

Chiefy reached me in three big steps and picked me up, just like I was a baby.

I put my arms around his neck, and before I could stop myself I began to cry.

12

How It All Happened

George saw me cry. And Frances Bird. And Gloria. And Candy. And when Chiefy let me down on the floor and I found my way to the ladies room with my Mom and came out to see them all there, I cried again. And when Mom and Dad and Gram all hugged me, I cried another time. And when they got me a hot dog with everything on it from the sandwich man, I cried once more. And the more I cried, the better I felt, so I kept on crying. That sure was a twerpy thing to happen, but it did.

The other things that happened were these:

Mr. Cigar, the auctioneer, was arrested by the state troopers who had come along with Chiefy and taken to a *real* jail. His helpers, who were "runners" at the auction (men who took money from the bidders and delivered their antiques to them), were arrested, too. I identified two of them as his partners in crime by their voices and by the fact that one of them ate lollipops and one of them chewed gum. Juicy Fruit. (Well, to be honest, George identified them, too.)

It was George—and Gloria—and Frances Bird who saved me from being auctioned off.

George, hiding in the closet, had disguised himself as a pile of old clothes. Wasn't that tee-rific? They never even noticed him on the floor of the closet. And when he heard the door slam and the truck drive off, he tried to open the closet door but found it only opened from the outside. He was locked in.

He screamed and screamed, but of course neither Gloria nor I was there to hear him. He finally figured that out. So what with the waiting and the dark and its being late at night, he fell asleep. If I hadn't done the same thing myself, I would have thought that was a dumb thing to do. But what else can you do in a closet—besides think and sleep?

Anyway, Gloria *did* get home. But she was tired and scared and didn't call Frances Bird until morning. Frances Bird made her call Chiefy.

And Chiefy and my parents raced over to the house. They found a lot of furniture gone—including the wardrobe, of course—and George asleep like a pile of old clothes on the closet floor.

Of course he had never seen the robbers, but he remembered their voices and imitated them. And he told his dad about the clues, just as Gloria and Frances Bird had.

Then Gloria remembered she had seen the truck. She described it as best she could.

And when they couldn't find me, not anywhere in the house, they figured I had been kidnapped. Or worse.

But Chiefy is a great detective. He figured out about auction houses right away because it's a fast way to get rid of furniture. In fact, Chiefy had already been checking out local auctions. He knew no respectable auctioneer would deal with stolen property, so he thought it might be someone who had his own auction house and was a bit shady and—smoked a cigar.

Only one man fit that description for a hundred miles around. His name was "Lester Gravel, the man with the Gavel." At least that's what he called himself. The state troopers had another name for him. "Fastest Gavel in the East."

So Chiefy and the state troopers raced down to the auction house. My folks and the kids were right behind. They found the auction already in progress.

When Chiefy saw the wardrobe closet going up for bid, he said he had a sudden impulse to buy it. At least, that's what he said. "Always wanted one of them things," was the way he put it. Later, he admitted that it was the only thing big enough for a kid to hide in, and if I was anywhere, that's where I'd be. Only he didn't know if I was dead or alive, and he didn't want to make a big scene and scare everyone, especially my Mom. And he was too far away to yell without Mr. Cigar—Mr. Gravel—getting away out the back door. So, he started bidding while signalling the troopers to move around back quietly, which they did.

Well, after the excitement quieted down, the five of us—Frances Bird, Gloria, Candy, George and me—were benched by our folks for a week.

"A whole week!" groaned George in school. But actually he didn't really mind because we were kind of heroes. And he was busy at school and on the phone telling all his buddies about his part in the thing, telling them everything except about becoming a girl, of course.

Frances Bird didn't seem to care that much either. She said, as we walked home from school, "I can get more homework done this way. Besides, we have that science project due next week."

"That's right," said Gloria, who was working with her.

Candy was the most hurt. After all, it meant no girl scouts on Monday, no piano lessons Tuesday, no ballet and tap Wednesday, no 4-H Thursday, and no drawing class Friday.

As for me, I was so glad to be home, I didn't mind at all. I would have plenty of time now—to plan our next case.

And so what if I can't sleep with the light out anymore? Sometimes you have to make sacrifices for a job well done.

And come to think of it, I'd be willing to sacrifice something more. My name. Don't you think Shirli is a real twerpy name for someone who is already a world-famous private eye?

Department of Public Instruction

San Rafael School Library
BAHIA VISTA SCHOOL

No._____

Marin County, California